Weekly Reader Children's Book Club presents

Wise Dog

Illustrated by *Lilian Obligado*

WISE DOG

By Josephine Wright

E. P. Dutton & Co., Inc.   New York

Also by Josephine Wright
COTTON CAT AND MARTHA MOUSE

Weekly Reader Children's Book Club Edition

Mitty and Matty were two little cats.

One day Mitty said to Matty,

"When I grow up I'll be in a circus."

"You, in a circus! What could you
do in a circus? They never have cats
in a circus."

"I'll not be a cat when I
grow up," said Mitty. "Anyone can
see that."

"Not be a cat?" asked Matty. "What
will you be?"

"I'll be a tiger. Can't you see
I'll grow up to be a tiger?"

Matty looked at Mitty.

"You do look something like
a tiger," she said. "I think
I'll be in a circus with you."

"You?" asked Mitty. "You just
said they never have cats in a circus.
What could you do in a circus?"

"I'll be an elephant,"
said Matty.

"Anyone can see that. Can't you see
I'll be an elephant when I grow up?"

"Yes, you do look something like
an elephant," said Mitty.

Just then the two cats saw
the monkey up in a tree.

"Good morning," Mitty and Matty
called out to the monkey.

11

The monkey came down from the tree.

"Good morning," he said. "What are you two little cats doing this fine morning?"

"Talking," said Mitty. "Do you know what I'll be when I grow up?"

"Yes, I do," said the monkey. "You will be just what you are now—a cat."

"Oh, no," said Mitty. "When I grow
up, I'll be much more important than
a cat. I'll be a tiger in a circus."

The monkey looked at Mitty.

"Well, well," he said. "So you will be
a tiger in a circus when you grow up,
will you?"

"Yes," answered Mitty. "Anyone can
see I'll be a tiger."

The monkey looked at Matty.

"What will you be when you grow up?"
he asked. "Will you be a tiger, too?"

"Oh, no," said Matty. "Can't you
see what I'll be? I'll be an elephant
in the circus. An elephant in a circus
is much more important than a cat."

"I see," said the monkey. "So you
will be an elephant and Mitty will
be a tiger."

"That is right," Matty told him.
"Mitty and I will be in the circus
when we grow up."

The monkey looked at the two little cats.
He was thinking.
At last he said to Mitty,
"If you are to be a tiger
when you grow up, you must
be a baby tiger now."

"Yes, that must be so," said Mitty.

Then the monkey looked at Matty.

"If you are to be an elephant

when you grow up, you must

be a baby elephant now."

"Yes, that must be so," said Matty.

"Then," asked the monkey, "why must you wait to grow up before you can be in a circus? Why not be in a circus now?"

"Oh! I'd like that," said Mitty.

"Oh! I'd like that, too," said Matty.

"Then come with me now, and you can be in my circus," said the monkey.

So Mitty and Matty went with the monkey.

But they did not know that the monkey
had no circus—no circus at all.

No, the monkey had no circus,
but he wanted to have one
and he knew how he could use
Mitty and Matty in a circus.

The monkey thought to himself,
"Mitty wants to be a tiger,
so I can use her for a tiger.
Matty wants to be an elephant,
so I can use her for an elephant.
They will think they are very important."

So the monkey put Mitty in a big cage
and closed the door.

He put Matty in a big cage and
closed the door.

"Now you are in a circus," the
monkey told them. Then he went away.

"Do you feel like a tiger in a cage?"
asked Matty.

"Oh, yes," said Mitty. "I feel
big, like a tiger. I feel much more
important than a cat. How about
you?"

"I feel much more important than
a cat, too," answered Matty. "I feel
big, just like an elephant."

All night long the two little cats
were happy in their cages.

In the morning the monkey said,
"Today we will start out. We will
stop here and there so all the animals
can see you. We will start right after
breakfast."

After breakfast the monkey started out
with the two cages.

As they rode along Mitty and Matty
looked out of their cages. "How big
and important we are!" they thought.

Later in the morning the monkey stopped near the home of his friend, the goat.

"Good morning, Mr. Goat," said the monkey. "Do you see my fine circus?"

The goat looked at Mitty and Matty in their cages.

"Is that your circus?" he asked.

"It is," said the monkey. "Will you
help me with my circus?"

"Yes, if I can," said the goat. "What
do you want me to do?"

"You have a good strong voice," said the
monkey. "Please call all the animals
to come and see my circus."

The goat did have a good strong voice
and he liked to use it.

"Come and see! Come and see!" called out
the goat. "See the big elephant. See the
big tiger! Come to the circus!"

All the animals came.

The rabbits came.
The cow came.

The horse came.

And the dog came, too.
The goat was already there.

But when the animals saw only Mitty and
Matty in the cages, they laughed.

"That is not a big tiger. That is only
a little cat," said the littlest rabbit.

Then the other animals called out,
"The littlest rabbit is right. That is
not a big elephant. That is only a
little cat," and they all laughed again.

The animals started home, laughing
as they went. The goat lay down
under one of the cages to rest his
strong voice, and the monkey climbed
up in a tree and went to sleep.

It was very still.

No one was looking at the monkey's circus—no one at all.

Mitty and Matty were unhappy. They did not feel important now. They did not like to be laughed at.

Mitty said, "In the morning we will go home. I do not like the circus."

"Yes, we will go home," said Matty. "The circus is not much fun."

Now the monkey was asleep, but the goat
was not.

He heard what Mitty and Matty said, and
the next morning he told his friend
the monkey.

The monkey said, "They think they will
go home, but I will not give up
my circus. I will not let them out of
their cages."

"That will be a good way to keep
them here," said the goat.

The monkey laughed. "They wanted
to be in a circus, and now they can
stay in the circus," he said.

Then the goat and the monkey went
off to eat their breakfast.

Soon the dog came back.

Now the dog was very wise. He was so
wise that all the animals called him
Wise Dog.

The dog saw that Mitty and Matty
were not happy. "The goat tells me
that you want to go home," said
Wise Dog, "but the monkey will not
let you out of your cages."

"That is right," said Matty. "He will
not open our cage doors. We can't
get out."

Wise Dog looked at Mitty and Matty.
He laughed to himself.
Then he said, "Let me think."
Wise Dog sat down.

"He's thinking," Mitty said to Matty.

"Yes, he's thinking," said Matty.

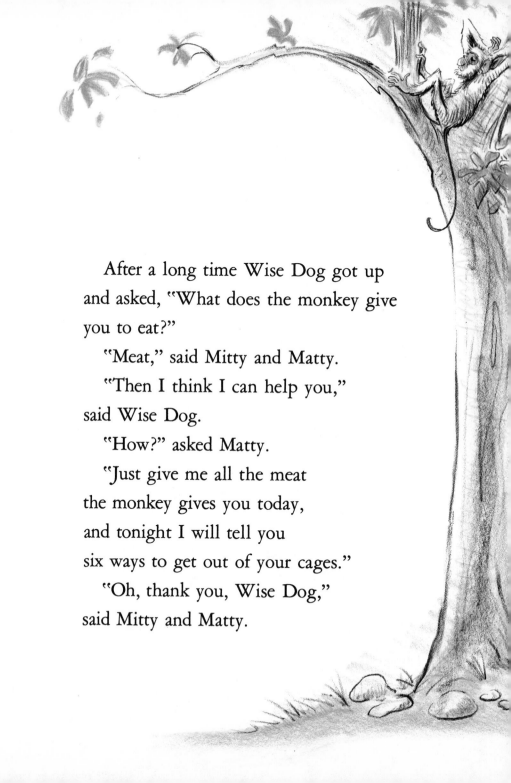

After a long time Wise Dog got up
and asked, "What does the monkey give
you to eat?"

"Meat," said Mitty and Matty.

"Then I think I can help you,"
said Wise Dog.

"How?" asked Matty.

"Just give me all the meat
the monkey gives you today,
and tonight I will tell you
six ways to get out of your cages."

"Oh, thank you, Wise Dog,"
said Mitty and Matty.

That night when the monkey
was asleep, Mitty and Matty gave
Wise Dog all their meat.

"Now," said Mitty, "tell us six ways
to get out of our cages."

Wise Dog put one foot up on Mitty's cage.

"You can just walk out," he said.

"You can walk out here, and here,
and here, and here, and here, and here."

"Oh, so we can," said Mitty. "How very
wise you are!" and she walked out
of her cage.

"How very, very wise you are," said Matty,
and she walked out of her cage.

"You can be wise, too," said the dog.
"How?" asked Mitty and Matty.

"Never again say you are a big tiger
or a big elephant," said Wise Dog.
"You are little cats, and if you
are wise you will say you are cats."

To this day Mitty and Matty are cats—
very wise cats.